THE ALPHABET GAME
56 PIECES OF EROTIC FLASH FICTION

Anna Sky, Charlie J Forrest & Lola Sparkles

The Kinky Brits

Copyright © 2015 by **Anna Sky, Charlie J Forrest & Lola Sparkles**

All rights reserved. No part of this publication may be reproduced, distributed or transmitted in any form or by any means, without prior written permission.

The Kinky Brits
http://thekinkybrits.com

Publisher's Note: This is a work of fiction. Names, characters, places, and incidents are a product of the author's imagination. Locales and public names are sometimes used for atmospheric purposes. Any resemblance to actual people, living or dead, or to businesses, companies, events, institutions, or locales is completely coincidental. All characters are above the age of 18. All trademarks and wordmarks used in this collection of fiction are the property of their respective owners.

Book Layout © 2015 SexyLittlePages.com

ISBN-13: 978-1515306627
ISBN-10: 1515306623

CONTENTS

THE CHALLENGE 1
   THE WORD LISTS 2
   LOLA SPARKLES 2
ANTICIPATION & AARDVARK 3
   ANTICIPATION BY ANNA SKY 3
   AARDVARK BY CHARLIE J FORREST 4
BREADSTICKS & BIBLIOPHILE 7
   BREADSTICKS BY ANNA SKY 7
   BIBLIOPHILE BY CHARLIE J FORREST 8
CLENCHY & CRUNCHY 11
   CLENCHY BY ANNA SKY 11
   CRUNCHY BY CHARLIE J FORREST 12
DRENCHED & DOOLALLY 15
   DRENCHED BY ANNA SKY 15
   DOOLALLY BY CHARLIE J FORREST 16
ECTOPLASM & EXTRANEOUS 19
   ECTOPLASM BY ANNA SKY 19
   EXTRANEOUS BY CHARLIE J FORREST 20
FIST & FISHING 23
   FIST BY ANNA SKY 23
   FISHING BY CHARLIE J FORREST 24
GOOSEBUMPS & GERONIMO 27

- GOOSEBUMPS BY ANNA SKY 27
- GERONIMO BY CHARLIE J FORREST 29
- HELD & HIGH-FIVE 31
  - HELD BY ANNA SKY 31
  - HIGH-FIVE BY CHARLIE J FORREST 33
- IMPRESSIVE (…MOST IMPRESSIVE) & IGLOO...35
  - IMPRESSIVE (…MOST IMPRESSIVE) BY ANNA SKY 35
  - IGLOO BY CHARLIE J FORREST 36
- JUDDERING & JOUSTING...39
  - JUDDERING BY ANNA SKY 39
  - JOUSTING BY CHARLIE J FORREST 40
- KNOCK KNOCK & KINETICS....................................43
  - KNOCK KNOCK BY ANNA SKY 43
  - KINETICS BY CHARLIE J FORREST 45
- LITTLE & LIPOSUCTION..49
  - LITTLE BY ANNA SKY 49
  - LIPOSUCTION BY CHARLIE J FORREST 50
- MÉNAGE & MUSHROOM...53
  - MÉNAGE BY ANNA SKY 53
  - MUSHROOM BY CHARLIE J FORREST 54
- INTERLUDE 57
- NOOOOOOOO! & NOROVIRUS.............................59
  - NOOOOOOOO! BY ANNA SKY 59
  - NOROVIRUS BY CHARLIE J FORREST 60
  - NOROVIRUS BY LOLA SPARKLES 62

- ORCHESTRATED & OMNISCIENT 63
  - ORCHESTRATED BY ANNA SKY 63
  - OMNISCIENT BY CHARLIE J FORREST 64
- PRESSED & PARAGON 67
  - PRESSED BY ANNA SKY 67
  - PARAGON BY CHARLIE J FORREST 68
  - PRESSED BY LOLA SPARKLES 69
- QUIM & QUINCE 73
  - QUIM BY ANNA SKY 73
  - QUINCE BY CHARLIE J FORREST 74
  - QUIM BY LOLA SPARKLES 76
- RESOURCEFUL & RA-RA SKIRT 79
  - RESOURCEFUL BY ANNA SKY 79
  - RA-RA SKIRT BY CHARLIE J FORREST 80
- SILENT & SANDPAPER 83
  - SILENT BY ANNA SKY 83
  - SANDPAPER BY CHARLIE J FORREST 84
- TREMBLING & TURTLE 87
  - TREMBLING BY ANNA SKY 87
  - TURTLE BY CHARLIE J FORREST 88
- UNDERGROUND & UGANDA 93
  - UNDERGROUND BY ANNA SKY 93
  - UGANDA BY CHARLIE J FORREST 94
- VIPERA BERUS & VOLVO 97
  - VIPERA BERUS BY ANNA SKY 97
  - VOLVO BY CHARLIE J FORREST 98

- WATCHERS & WART 101
  - WATCHERS BY ANNA SKY 101
  - WART BY CHARLIE J FORREST 102
- MARKS THE SPOT & XENOPLASTIC 105
  - MARKS THE SPOT BY ANNA SKY 105
  - XENOPLASTIC BY CHARLIE J FORREST 106
- YODELLING & YIDDISH 109
  - YODELLING BY ANNA SKY 109
  - YIDDISH BY CHARLIE J FORREST 110
  - YIDDISH BY LOLA SPARKLES 111
- ZENITH & ZOOCHOROUS 113
  - ZENITH BY ANNA SKY 113
  - ZOOCHOROUS BY CHARLIE J FORREST 115
- THE KINKY BRITS 118
  - ANNA SKY 118
  - CHARLIE J FORREST 119
  - LOLA SPARKLES 119

INTRODUCTION

THE CHALLENGE

In the interests of trying to make Charlie lose yet another bet, Anna decided to bet him to the June Spanking A to Z Blog Challenge…

> *26 blog posts, one per day in June each starting with a new letter of the alphabet i.e. we'd have to start tomorrow. You up for it? We need to agree a min. word limit and the penalty ;)*

The actual rules can be found at http://spankingromance.com/june-challenge-spanking-a-to-z-spanka2z/, but we added a few extra twists...

1) Each participant provides the other with a list of words, beginning A, B, C etc...

2) Each participant must post their entry on this website in the #spankAtoZ category by midnight each night, using the assigned word in their story.

3) Each entry must be at least 250 words and a piece of flash fiction (also bear in mind that we are going for quantity not quality here).

4) If either party loses, they will receive 50 cane strikes...ouch...! Anna's will be administered by Mr Sky and Charlie's by Anna (or her nominated substitute).

THE WORD LISTS

We swapped words at 10pm on the 4th June – not much time for the first story to be written. Anna and Mr Sky schemed a wonderful list to push Charlie's writing and sanity as far as they could. Charlie missed the opportunity to do the same and provided Anna with a lovely list to work with!

LOLA SPARKLES

Lola came a little later to the Kinky Brits Challenge – she'd become sick of hearing Charlie complain about his words and thought **norovirus** really *wasn't* a challenge. She wrote a few stories using Charlie's words, just to rub a bit of salt in ;)

A IS FOR...

ANTICIPATION & AARDVARK

ANTICIPATION BY ANNA SKY

Anna waited in anticipation of the word list. It had been a risk, challenging Charlie like that, particularly as she was sure she'd lost the last bet which meant 50 strikes with the white springy cane across her bare buttocks. She winced as she thought about the impact of each one; each hit would bite into her flesh and Mr Sky would slowly ramp up the pressure to force her to her limits.

She giggled a bit though as she read back through the list she and Mr Sky had created for Charlie to use. It was pure evil genius and she hoped he wasn't returning the favour. Would he use her favourite topics to write about, like spanking and ropes and lovely kinky things? Perhaps his words would give her the freedom to write the flash fiction where inspiration struck. Allow the words to flow naturally rather than being forced. Not like her list. No, that would be hard to get into a writing flow with. Especially for 26 consecutive days...

She had happy thoughts, perhaps Charlie wouldn't finish the challenge and she'd get to exact her revenge upon him. It was partly his fault of course, goading her with phrases like "I'm kind of doubting you have it in you to administer said penalties". He was wrong. Oh, so wrong. She might practise her backswing, but that would require a bit of effort. She'd had a much better idea...she'd delegate the task to a seasoned pro, someone who'd really give him what for...

AARDVARK BY CHARLIE J FORREST

"You can't be serious," I said.

"Look, you agreed to this and what I'm saying is completely within the rules. Of course if you want to back out now then that's fine," she said. Her grin said a dozen or so silent words; words that referred to that evil little device of misery he knew for a fact she had hung up on a rack in her bedroom.

"But this is hardly fair. I mean, even if not a violation of the letter of the rules it's a clear breach of the spirit of the damned thing!"

"Look why in the hell are you griping. I actually think you've got this the wrong way around. I mean how much harm can it actually do?"

"Are you kidding me? Have you read up on these things? Have you any idea how many different kinds of horrific life-threatening infections I'll get if that thing lays its claws on me."

"Enough! You said you were prepared to wrestle a wild animal, so here we are."

"Well we could argue on the wild aspec–"

"Is it at home on somebody's sofa?" she snapped.

"No, bu–"

"Well then it's a wild animal. Now stop lollygagging and get your hairy backside in there!"

It wasn't hard. They don't really bother putting animals like this behind proper fencing.

Not like the lions and tigers and elephants. Fuck it ever since the Belfast incident you can't even get to the penguins as easily as this.

The concrete of the pen smacks into the soles of my feet. It's rough and, glancing up, the walls seem a lot taller from this side. I immediately regret the decision to go through with this. There's a rustling sound to my left. I try not to squeal as I look that way. It's already there, long furry snout protruding from behind an imitation concrete rock. Its beady little eyes blink at me. Then it comes charging. I manage to dodge the claws for the most part but it's a battle already lost. In less time than it takes to eat a Magnum whilst heckling an overweight man being assaulted by an exotic animal, the creature had me pinned to the floor. And my thought, my last, stubborn thought before it slips its long, probing tongue into places that should never be tongued, is this:

There really are no lengths I won't go to in the interest of a good spanking.

"Fucking aardvarks!" I muttered as the tongue crept into my ear.

B IS FOR...

BREADSTICKS & BIBLIOPHILE

BREADSTICKS BY ANNA SKY

It had been a long time since we'd been out on a date. They say familiarity breeds contempt and that wasn't quite true, but we had fallen into a comfortable groove. We had a regular routine, and over time even the sex had become formulaic. It went from wild and passionate and raw to more of a comfort blanket. It had moved from the physical into my head; in there anything could happen but externally, I could predict it down to the last thrust.

And now we sat in a fancy restaurant, trying to grab back what we were missing. We sat in comfortable silence that was tinged with awkwardness. Our familiarity with each other felt out of place, out of context when surrounded by black-tie waiters, flickering candles and grissini breadsticks.

I plucked one from the jar on the table, absent-mindedly swirling it into the olive oil and balsamic vinegar. I tentatively licked the end, wanting to know how sticky rich the balsamic was and how the olive oil coated my tongue before committing to a full bite.

He looked at me though, just a glance and that was enough. I slid the stick into my mouth, sucking it like a naughty schoolgirl would a lollipop, and held his gaze, defying him not to look away. He didn't. His eyes moved synchronously with my up-and-down motion, and I felt the hem of my skirt being lifted. His fingertips ghosted imperceptible circles up my inner thigh, promising what was to come.

He leant in, conspiratorially. "Just wait till I get you home…"

BIBLIOPHILE BY CHARLIE J FORREST

It can get spooky sometimes, in the hidden places. Places where you aren't really supposed to be. Places where you feel like you're only there by the grace of… something. Something that lurks in the dark corners. Or perhaps by grace of the darkness itself.

The fluorescent bulbs say hello in their own secret language, fluttering into life with little cries of "Blink!"

You weren't supposed to be here. I could feel the edges creeping in around us as we walked.

You already had a bad reputation. The other librarians spotted you as soon as your ID code cropped up on the system. They used to pass your items to me with unspoken urges of "please deal with him!"

And when the items came back, stained and frayed and dog-eared everyone would encourage me to log a complaint. But I didn't, instead I patched our precious legacy together with sellotape and lust.

"Take me," I'd think as I passed you some priceless manuscript. "Break my spine like a first edition of Eliphas Levi. Drop spittle and careless ink on my pages, then toss me aside and boast to your friends how you're better than them. How you don't truly understand me until you've read me in the original French.

That's why I brought you down here. A careless vandal in the archives. I can feel the volumes bristle, violated by your presence.

It's a confusion of terms, "bibliophile" as if to love a book means putting it on a pedestal like a god. I don't want that sort of love. I want the love of broken beautiful things. The love that grasps the present with a ferocity that devours, smudges and fingerprints and to hell with ISBNs.

C IS FOR...

CLENCHY & CRUNCHY

CLENCHY BY ANNA SKY

I don't know what it was, perhaps the look in his eye or his tone of voice. It triggered something inside me, like a switch had been flipped. I gripped my thighs together to quell the fluttering in my cunt; I felt clenchy, the first time in a long time that he'd caused me to feel this way.

His fingertips gripped tighter between my thighs, a warning. I clenched again, this was a side of him I'd not seen before and I liked it. "Whatever will you do to me?" I mock pouted and looked up at him through my eyelashes, playing the naughty schoolgirl once more.

"Keep on behaving like that and I might spank you." There was a gentle cough and we both looked up, startled, to see a waiter, straight-faced like he'd not heard us. We'd been so involved in our few seconds of fantasy, we'd forgotten where we were.

"I'll have the steak please, rare." I tried to keep the wobble out of my voice, my pussy throbbing almost uncontrollably with need. All around us people continued to eat, and I felt totally out of place. Surely they could see my flushed face and smell my rising heat?

"Skipping the starter, love?" His voice was full of amusement as he gripped my thigh again. I nearly jumped, all my nerve endings sensitised to his touch.

"Yeah, I'm not as hungry as I thought." Oh but I was hungry, hungry for him, for what he could do to me. I wriggled in my chair and took a deep breath. Tonight was going to be far more interesting than I'd previously thought.

CRUNCHY BY CHARLIE J FORREST

"What did it feel like?" he asked, breathless.

"I, I don't know," I lied.

The truth was, it was terrifying. In a moment I'd gone from happy, engaged, and joyfully aroused to a shivering, naked vulnerable thing.

"Are you ok?" he asked.

I shook my head, or tried to, I got about half way through the movement before he was against me, my cheek pressed firmly against his chest, his arms crushing me to him. I cried. I didn't mean to, and a part of me insisted on mumbling apologies even as the tears flowed. But he just smiled, and brushed a hand over my hair and told me it was alright.

Later, much later, we talked. After some sleep, and crap television, and lengthy debate over who had to leave the bed to answer the door for the pizza delivery.

"It was like," I said, unsure of how to crowbar the conversation back to that moment, when I was still trembling and lost in the woods. "It was like you broke something–No, not like that!" I said hurriedly, trying to calm the look of panic on his face. "I don't mean it in a bad way. But it's like, like when you crack into an egg, or eat a crème brûlée. You have to break into it, it's the whole nature of the thing. Some things can't be perfect or they'll never be any use to anyone."

"You're saying I broke you, but in a good way?"

"Yes, I guess I am, but it's not just a good thing, it's an essential thing. Imagine you're a dragon, in an egg."

"Ok."

"You have all this potential, you can be an incredible, beautiful creature. But whilst the egg is perfect, your wings can't fly."

"Is that a song lyric?" he asked.

"No."

"It sounds like a song lyric."

"Well it's not."

"Are you lying there quoting some emo rock singer at me?"

"He's not emo he's heavy metal, old school, and his solo work is massively underrated!" I said.

He didn't reply, only grinning. I thumped him in the shoulder. He responded in the way I'd secretly hoped, grasping my upper arms in his hands, twisting me round, pinning me to the bed.

"Break me again," I think to myself, "crack open my shell again and again until it's tiny, crunchy pieces underfoot. Set me free, free to fly, free to breathe fire!"

D IS FOR...

DRENCHED & DOOLALLY

DRENCHED BY ANNA SKY

I didn't taste much of dinner; I'm sure he didn't either. We skipped dessert too, opting to hustle ourselves into a taxi and get home quicker. Neither of us said a word in the back of the cab. All the while his fingers pressed insistently into my thighs, alternately squeezing then relaxing. He looked straight ahead, but when I looked down at his crotch, appearing as it did in the street lights before disappearing again into the darkness, he was definitely aroused.

I was too, the steady strum that I felt in my pussy hadn't left. It was a reminder of how we used to be before the routine set in, and I liked the feeling. I remembered how just the sight of him made me pulse and throb, how I nearly melted when he kissed me deep and hard, and how we spent hours fucking; we'd be drenched in sweat and the room would be steeped in the smell of sex. Perhaps tonight would end like that too. I wanted it, and right now, I wanted it with him.

I leant in, feeling his slight stubble graze against my cheek. I breathed in deeply, holding the memories in place and trying to make new ones. He turned slightly to kiss me, it was the merest nudge with his lips to the top of my head. His hand slid up my thigh, fingers grazing over the thin cotton of my knickers and I inhaled reflexively. Holding my breath seemed the right thing to do. It held me in the moment. And then his other hand reached round, pulling my face up to meet his, fingers hooked under my jaw.

There was no uncertainty in the movement, no hesitation and it didn't leave room for regret or what-ifs. His lips met mine, again the merest of touches. I whimpered slightly, easing towards him, cursing the restraint of the seat belt. But he backed off.

"I told you to wait until I got you home." He admonished me gently, swirling one fingertip so tantalisingly over my clit. I gritted my teeth, that wasn't how I interpreted what he'd said earlier; I thought he just wanted to get into my knickers, not to make me a hot, desperate mess.

DOOLALLY BY CHARLIE J FORREST

With hindsight I shouldn't have been surprised to find Bert where I did. His irrepressible wit and omnipresent smile could never really hide the fact that, for all his good intentions, he was basically unemployable. In the short spell of my last trip he had swung wildly from busking to street art, finally culminating in sweeping chimneys. But it would seem that even this wasn't sufficient to keep him toeing the straight and narrow.

The place was a fug of smoke as I entered. Handkerchief to my nose. Yet I could feel myself getting light-headed even so. I tried to focus my mind on thinking where it was I first heard about such places. Yes, that's right, it's in one of those Sherlock Holmes stories, begins the very same way in fact.

I scanned the room in a hurry. Hoping that I wouldn't find him. Or that, perhaps if I did a cursory enough job it would somehow prevent him from being there. But it wasn't enough. He was in the far corner, sprawled amidst a mass of bodies, one leg tucked up, lanky and thin. Oh Bert, even off your face and half destitute you still managed to do it in a way that looked oh so cocky. Except, when I reached the face, that all changed. I could see him now without the mask for the first time. A mass of confusion and regret.

Once I got him outside into the sunshine something of his old self came back. He looked at me and, even without the mask of jollity there was a light in his eyes. A light that sparked memories of that night years ago. While the rest of them were flying kites on the common he took me up to the roof. We sat, perched on the ridge of tiles watching the sun go down.

"You know what I love about our society?" he whispered in my ear.

"No, what?"

"It's that, even though we pretend we're so civilised, even though you can put skirt over skirt over skirt around your legs, there's no getting away from the reality of the situation…"

His arm was across my chest, flinging me back onto the far side of the roof, out of sight of anyone.

"…no matter how many skirts you wear, it's still so easy to have you open and ready for me," he said. His hand brushing up my leg, tossing back my covering layers. He'd probably been expecting something, a pair of bloomers perhaps, but I think I knew his game better than he did, when his hand reached the top of my thigh and found nothing, not even a wisp of silk to bar his path. Not that he'd acknowledge it. Oh no, Bert, oh so fucking cocky Bert just pretended he knew I was knickerless under those layers. But I knew, I knew by the gleam in his eye as we came together, I knew he was impressed.

"You must think me right proper doolally to have done this to meself," he said.

I pulled him close, his face into my shoulder so I didn't have to look him in the eye. Instead I watched the leaves blow left to right, then right to left. Time to be going.

E IS FOR...

ECTOPLASM & EXTRANEOUS

ECTOPLASM BY ANNA SKY

We'd first met at the university. He was a cellular biologist studying crap-only-knows-what for his PhD and I was attempting my Master's in biology, spending lots of time in the great outdoors. Normally I wouldn't have gone for someone like him, but he was so impressed when I didn't immediately break into the Ghostbusters theme tune when he mentioned he worked with ectoplasm, that he asked me out on a date and I found myself saying 'yes'.

The rest as they is history. The taxi pulled up outside our Edwardian terrace. Matt, ever the perfect gentleman, opened the door for me and helped me out. And then he wasn't gentlemanly any more. He gripped my elbow and I was suddenly propelled up the few steps to the front door almost faster than I could keep up. I don't know how we got inside, but I was pressed up against the tiles of the hallway, cold ceramic against my cheek.

He pushed down into me. I think I heard him kick the door closed but I was caught in a surreal moment. His mouth was on me, attacking me. I could barely breathe yet he carried on, twisting one hand into my hair to hold me in place. His other hand was warm and almost painful against my neck; I was going nowhere.

He thrust his crotch against mine, and I felt like I were going to explode into a million pieces. How I didn't is beyond me. His tongue pushed against mine, his lips bruised and he plundered my mouth for all I had. His hand left my throat and worked into my coat, removing it with force. I didn't hear it hit the floor, I was all consumed by his fire and need for me. He worked his way into my top, lifting my breasts out of my bra, so they were just supported by the cups and wiring. All the while he was kissing, bruising, wanting.

My breasts were small as he squeezed them in his hands, my nipples rigid nubs as he pinched and pulled at them. I couldn't suppress a moan and tried to grind against him, but he had me pinned, exactly where he wanted me.

EXTRANEOUS BY CHARLIE J FORREST

There are times when it really pays to take the initiative. This was definitely one of those. Sweat prickling over his skin, eyes glazed over, breath ragged. I pulled away from him a little, taking his hand in mine, rolling away from him and pulling him tight around me like a cloak. He squirmed a little, thrusting one arm out beneath my neck, the other draping around me from above. He didn't need me to tell him to squeeze, to pull me against him, to whisper a bizarre thoughtless combination of compliments and lewd suggestions in my ear.

I held him back of course, my arms scooping up to hold his, like a tyrannosaur clutching a baby.

"You know," he whispered.

"What?"

"I like this, but I always feel like there's one arm too many."

"Would you rather have it chopped off?" I asked.

"Perhaps, but only if it meant we could stay like this forever."

He couldn't see my grin, but I squeezed his hands extra hard to make up for it. I planted a kiss on the arm that passed underneath, thought for a moment.

"No, we couldn't possibly chop this arm off," I said.

"Why not?"

"Well it's hardly fair, depriving me of my favourite sex toy."

I couldn't see his grin, but he squeezed me extra tight, his cock growing hard again, pressed tight between my buttocks.

"It does feel a little extraneous," he said.

"What feels extraneous?"

"My arm, I mean are you honestly telling me I need both of them to please your wanton desires?"

My mind flits back to what we did earlier that evening, one hand grasping my hair, pulling me back against him while the other parted my thighs.

"I think I can tolerate a certain amount of extraneousness," I said.

F IS FOR...

FIST & FISHING

FIST BY ANNA SKY

He continued twisting my hair in his fist and pulled me forwards. The cold air on my naked breasts sent a shiver through me but Matt didn't seem to notice.

"Upstairs." His voice was tight with tension and he tugged harder, urging me to follow. The pain in my scalp as he pulled was a strange sensation, wrong yet so right. I climbed the stairs awkwardly after him, my head pinned at an angle; my whole body throbbed in anticipation.

He dragged me into the bedroom and threw me onto the bed. I felt light-headed, his sudden release of me had caught me by surprise. I leant back to take a deep breath but he pounced, surprisingly delicately, onto me. I lay between his thighs; he squeezed them at my hips, my own thighs pressed together and my hands trapped against my body.

He had one hand on my throat, holding me to the bed. "You like this, don't you?" He growled. "And to think I never knew it, you dirty little whore." I was shocked, this wasn't the Matt I knew and I felt my cheeks colour in embarrassment. But somewhere deep down, his words spoke to me, hot-lining to my cunt and making it throb all the more.

"Well?"

I hesitated. He increased the pressure slightly on my throat and looked at me expectantly. "Yes," I replied.

"Yes what?"

"Yes, I like it. I don't know what you're doing to me but I like it. I want it."

Matt released his hand and I took the deep breath that I needed. He stood up, and pulled me to my feet.

"Get undressed," he said.

FISHING BY CHARLIE J FORREST

It was a windy day, the kind of windy day where it becomes a question of when, not if, you pack up your kit and get the hell off the pier for fear of being swept out to sea. In short, a typical day for fishing.

Spray was forming a near permanent haze and it felt as if parts of my body had forgotten what it felt like to be dry. To try and keep my spirits up I fell into conversation with the man next to me.

"What I don't get," I said after some strange twist of conversation got us talking about myths. "Is what's so alluring about a mermaid? I mean, so far as I can tell you're not gonna be able to have much fun at all unless you like grinding against a load of scales."

"You think that's bad, imagine what it must be like for her."

"How do you mean?"

"Well, being that way, caught between two worlds, too slow and strange for the fish, too... ill-equipped for the tastes of most humans."

Something in the way he formed his words told me there was more to this tale. I pressed him and he span a yarn about one summer when he was on a quiet island-hopping trip in the speckly bits of Greece, those hundreds of tiny uninhabited islands between the mainland and the Mediterranean.

"I set off from the others, believin' there'd be better prospects on the south side. Took me an hour or more to get there, scrabbling round the rocks. Looking for a nice spot. I also got this impression, like I was a classical hero, stepping on stone no man had touched in thousands of years. Truth be told it barely caught me by surprise when I came around an outcrop and saw her there, sprawled on the sand a little below the high tide mark."

"Now what they don't tell you in all the old stories is that the tail, that huge, lithe tail, is pretty much entirely muscle. So yes, she beckoned me over, but I was in no doubt, if she wanted to, she could give one swish of that tail and thud. That'd be the end of my story. British holiday maker dies under unusual circumstances."

"See, she was waving to me, but the look in her eye it was heart-breaking, a mixture of desire and despair. And I knew then, just as sure as I'm talking to you, I knew just what she wanted, how tortured a creature she must be. So I did all I could. I sat next to her on the sand, tracing my finger along her jaw, guiding her lips to mine. She tasted of salt and air and pebbles. I stroked a hand down her shoulder, pulling her body against mine, each moment wondering whether something I did would go wrong and bring that mighty tail to crush me into oblivion."

"She moaned as I moved to her breasts, crushing them between me and her, my hand snaking in between to pinch her nipples as our lips limply bit at each other. But I'll tell you this for nothing, it was her neck that did it. When I nuzzled my face between her jaw and shoulder, kissing, sucking, nibbling, that's when her breath caught in her throat, that's when the great tail thrashed and juddered."

"And what happened then?" I asked.

"Well then she kissed me again, breathless, and in another moment she was gone."

A wave finally broke, as in bodily broke, over the side of the pier, sending my cool box off, away and through between the rails. I dove after but it was too late. Reality snapped back and I kicked myself for believing things too easily when, just for a moment, I thought I saw a hand reaching into the box as it sank, followed by a great tail just beneath the foam.

G IS FOR...

GOOSEBUMPS & GERONIMO

GOOSEBUMPS BY ANNA SKY

I slowly took off my clothes, feeling like a specimen under Matt's microscope. He looked at me with an odd intensity as I peeled away first my blouse, and then my skirt. Goosebumps formed on my skin. It wasn't cold but I shivered slightly all the same; Matt's sudden change in behaviour and his intense focus left me feeling blindsided and I needed some thinking space.

My skirt dropped to the floor, and I kicked off my shoes. Now I was down to my underwear. I struggled to look up at Matt; part of me was ashamed that he could make me feel this way so easily whilst another part felt so fucking alive that I didn't want him to see. I didn't want it to end.

"And the rest." His voice was suddenly harsh, cutting across my cocoon of thoughts.

"Make me!" I shot back at him, without even thinking of the consequences.

He grabbed my wrist and twisted me down over his knee as he sat on the edge of the bed. I felt suddenly vulnerable, my bottom over his thighs and my arms and legs dangling down either side. He pushed down into my back and I felt my bra strap loosen as he unfastened it. He slowly worked my knickers down over his thighs and my entire body tensed in response.

He stroked his hands down my back, a feather light touch from the nape of my neck to the curve of my buttocks. His hands were warm on my cooler skin and I shivered again but not from cold.

"What happened?" I asked him quietly. I didn't want this to stop but I had to know why we'd gone from boring routine to something that was quite frankly, very hot and very, as far as I knew, kinky.

He continued to run his hands over me as he spoke. "I read that damn book that everyone had been banging on about. The one with the tie on the cover?" I didn't need to look at Matt to know he was smiling, most likely from nerves. "And I liked some of the ideas, so I did some more reading on the internet and worked out how to do it properly."

I could have laughed then, but I didn't. We'd both done the same thing, only he was braver than me; he'd done something about it.

Matt continued, the smile gone from his voice. His hand came to rest on my buttocks. "I'm going to spank you now."

GERONIMO BY CHARLIE J FORREST

He likes challenges. Likes playing with my head, evoking emotions so strong they want to rip me apart, then conjuring something different, until I'm bleary eyed and whimpering from the confusion. Two dragons, yes, two dragons fighting over my mind.

Because he can do that, turn things on their head because I let him, because I want him to. Tell me black is white and he has six fingers and I swear if he has me where he wants me I'll say it's so and I'll believe it. Because there are times when a fantasy, his fantasy, really are better than anything reality can conjure.

It started off with simple things, little hints. Like the times he'd pull funny faces during sex, daring me to break down and giggle and if I did, oh if I did he'd flip me onto my front, his palm dancing furiously over my buttocks until I was squealing in a mix of delight and agony.

He comes into the room with a grin on his face. His cock swings lazily from side to side, half erect. He reaches out a hand, grasping my hair in his fist. I let my mouth drop open, automatically stretching it wider than I ever would for the dentist. My tongue slides over my bottom teeth, a red carpet for his royal hardness.

"Geronimoooo!" he cries. Confused, distracted, I open my eyes, and try to look up at him. His cock catches me off guard, bouncing against my tongue. I fight down the instinct to cough, splutter, trying to focus on taking him in, moving my head, lips, tongue the way he likes, while my senses are still ringing. Eyes bleary.

And all I can think is, "is this what he means by head-fuck?"

H IS FOR...

HELD & HIGH-FIVE

HELD BY ANNA SKY

There was a strange twisting sensation in my belly at Matt's words and a thousand thoughts rushed through my head. *Would it hurt? Would I like it?* I felt ridiculous too, held over his knee as I was, arse beneath his hand.

He rubbed at my buttocks and I felt, as well as heard, him breathe deeply. His whole body shifted slightly and I imagined him gearing up to start. Perhaps he was having similar, corresponding feelings to my own. Matt was gentle and sweet, he didn't believe violence solved anything and here I was over his knee about to receive his hand across my bottom. Disappointment crept in to my thoughts, *what if he couldn't do it?* Oops, there it was. I wanted him to spank me.

The warmth of his palm suddenly moved off my skin and I flinched, hearing his hand sweep through the air. It didn't hurt as his hand landed though. And then he did it again and again. It made my skin tingle and I wiggled against his thighs in anticipation.

"Stay still," he hissed. I tried not to giggle but I couldn't help it; I knew the look of concentration that would be on his face, the slight frown that would appear, creasing between his eyes.

"And stop that too!" His hand came down harder this time and it stung slightly. The sensation travelled through to my clit, swollen with need and I thrust my hips down harder on Matt's leg. He pushed down hard into the small of my back, pinning me down in response to my movement. I took a deep breath, perhaps now was not the time to be giggling.

I was right. I'd triggered something in Matt and whereas he was barely touching me before, he now spanked harder, covering every inch of my bottom. The rounded, fleshier part wasn't so bad but when he found the sensitive area at the point where my bottom met my thighs, I squealed. He spanked me there over and over.

"Please, please Matt." The words fell out of my mouth as I writhed beneath him, wanting him to stop but not wanting him to stop. Everything was a curious rush of sensation and I didn't know what to do with myself. I think Matt realised I'd had enough as he slowed down to a gentle tap again, before stroking my back in long, deep, massaging motions.

"Are you ok, Fi?" he asked cautiously.

"Yeah, I think so." I tried to stand up but was shaking. My whole body felt really sensitive all of a sudden. I felt our fleecy blanket being wrapped around my shoulders and Matt helped steady me as I collapsed on to the bed.

He held me tight, using his hold body to pin me, chrysalis-like, until the shaking subsided. He stroked my hair out of my face and kissed my forehead and I felt as though I were floating.

HIGH-FIVE BY CHARLIE J FORREST

Anna's note: This is where Charlie actually FAILS the challenge (he didn't use 'high five' in the story itself), but I didn't tell him, just in case I needed ammunition later on ;)

I spot him as soon as he gets on the train, lithe body wriggling between the other passengers. A practiced awkward shuffle that gets him deep inside the carriage away from the scrum by the doors. He's a pretty sort, dark curly hair atop a soft, structured face. High cheek bones and a long neck. He has that sort of in-between body and pale skin that's just asking to have mean things done to it.

His hair is dishevelled, clothes too crumpled for so early in the morning. I catch his eye as he glances around, but he doesn't respond. His gaze is lost far away. And then, as the train pulls into another station, the woman opposite me stands up. She shuffles past him and he sinks into her seat. Nobody else on the train is watching, nobody else on the train spots the little wince as his buttocks kiss the hard cushion.

I don't know why they call it the walk of shame. I mean yes I know, deep down I know, that it comes from the same place as that look of anguished embarrassment. The same place that tells him he's wrong for wanting what he wants, for needing what he needs.

Oh how I wish I could have been a fly on the wall, or maybe I just wish I could go to him, wrap my arms around him and whisper in his ear. Tell him he's been a good boy, that it's all fine, and that the feeling squirming away in his chest is actually a sort of happiness he's never let himself feel before.

But I don't manage this. Life in the city seems to put some gestures beyond reach. But as the train pulls into my station I catch his eye again. Holding his gaze I shuffle awkwardly to my feet and, in the moments before the doors slide open, present my hand for him, palm forwards. He slaps it gently and the squirming in his chest reaches up to tweak his lips into a grin. A grin he'll have for the rest of the day.

I IS FOR...

IMPRESSIVE (...MOST IMPRESSIVE) & IGLOO

IMPRESSIVE (...MOST IMPRESSIVE) BY ANNA SKY

I don't know how long we lay there for but I felt warm and safe in Matt's arms. I was curious how my bottom looked though and got up to have a look. In my mind, my backside was flaming mess of red hand-prints; it felt hot and bruised, like it was radiating heat.

Matt sat up to watch as I twisted and turned in front of the mirror, trying to get the best view.

"Impressive...very impressive," I muttered as I looked. It wasn't quite how I expected, whilst there were a couple of more distinct marks, it was the mottled bruising got my attention.

The whole area was dark pink, and there were little flecked patches all over. They were individual tiny marks, not the huge bruises I expected but I'd never seen myself decorated like this before.

"Let's have a look." Matt stood behind me, and I watched him in the mirror, running his hands over me. There was something incredibly erotic about seeing his hands move over my breasts and pinching my nipples. He curved his hands over my waist and stomach and I breathed in as he did so, a habit I've always had.

He slapped my bottom in warning, although he was much gentler this time. "You're beautiful exactly as you are," he said, and turned my face so I met his eye in the reflection.

His hands continued down my body, massaging and squeezing until they found all the sensitive spots on my bottom. I wriggled beneath his touch, finding it painful yet arousing at the same time.

Matt turned me round to face him and gripping me tightly, kissed me hard on the mouth. It was just like old times, the familiar light-headed feeling flooded back. I gasped in relief and pleasure, and leant in for more.

IGLOO BY CHARLIE J FORREST

"This is not a fucking igloo!"

"Yes it is."

"No, seriously," he said, "in what possible universe can you call this an igloo?"

"It's made of ice; QED."

"Don't you QED me, this is completely different."

"How?"

"Well two reasons, first is that technically, as the ice was here first this is more of an excavation whereas an igloo is a structure a–"

"–boring!"

He grabs my hand, twisting my wrist with a snarl. My arm locks up, spinning me away from him. His free hand snakes around my front. Sometimes he likes to grip my by the neck, I love it when he does that. But not this time.

His fingers pinch the zip fastener of my fleece, dragging it down inch after angry inch. He palms the fabric aside, reaching for my waist, grasping the bottom of my under layers. He releases my hand, but before I can pull free he's tugged all three layers off over my head leaving me hunched over half naked. He tosses the clothes aside, they skid into a far corner, too far to reach. Then he comes for me. I try to run, which can be risky at the best of times.

My shoes refuse to make friends with the ice and I slam heavily onto my buttocks. I blink, recognising the pain, knowing that he'll stop in a moment if I show it, covering my grimace I'm off, scrabbling across the floor. It doesn't last for long and soon I feel his reassuring weight crushing my chest into the icy floor of the ice-hotel.

"Second, is that in a space this size you might be able to get away… but only might."

J IS FOR...

JUDDERING & JOUSTING

JUDDERING BY ANNA SKY

Matt took my wrists in his hands, and held them behind my back. He kissed me again and I closed my eyes, breathing deeply.

Despite the aftermath of the spanking, I was still turned on and was now feeling horny. Matt read me well. He pinned both my wrists in one hand, whilst the other pinched playfully at my buttocks. The bruised feeling had subsided but they were still sensitive and I tried to move away from his ministrations. He didn't let me though, pulling me towards him and letting me know he was in charge.

He pulled me back down to the bed, pinching and kissing and keeping me turned on. Whenever I tried to wriggle or move out of his grasp he held me tighter; there was no escape.

Once on the bed he straddled me, and grinning, he pulled a silvery grey tie out from under the pillow. I must have looked like the proverbial bunny in the headlights as he winked, and tied my wrists tightly above my head. "I told you," he said. "I read the book with the tie on the cover!"

I moaned, all my tension trying to leave my body in that one long exhalation. Matt secured the tie to the bed head and I realised he'd trapped me; I was now completely at his mercy.

He moved down my body, alternating long strokes with his hands for gentle swats. His tongue followed, trailing down my torso and nibbling and biting when I least expected it. My breath came harder and faster and when he finally reached my clit, my body was almost juddering with anticipation.

JOUSTING BY CHARLIE J FORREST

Condom condom burning bright, in the shadows of the night

What immortal hand or eye could face thy fearful symmetry?

"What was that?"

"Oh, nothing just… my brain got away from me a bit there."

"Good, because you do realise this is serious business, I mean we're not just doing this for fun y'know."

I stifle a laugh. "No, of course not."

I sit up on the bed, shuffling the cushions into a more comfortable sitting position, then reach for the light switch. It takes a while for our eyes to grow accustomed to the glow. We closed the metal shutter over the window so tight, so very tight that we may as well be underground. I even insisted we put the snake-shaped draught excluder at the foot of the door to keep the corridor light from interrupting us.

It's as if my eyes are slowly reaching into the darkness, picking up on faint traces of things close to me, then a little further and a little further away. After five minutes or so I can make out the pair of them, kneeling at the foot of the bed. I raise my arm and let the white handkerchief, the brightest thing in the dim room, drop to the blanket in front of me.

"Let the jousting begin."

"I thought this was a duel?"

"Whatever," I say, "begin!"

There's a rip of foil, then two blobs of gentle phosphorescence decorate the night, bobbing in invisible hands, stretching, growing into a pair of disembodied cocks. The bed creaks as they move closer together. When they're almost touching there's a pause, a silence of anticipation. Without being told my tongue strokes across my lips, wondering who will be the victor, who will be the first I get my hands on. The red, or the green.

"We meet again at last," comes a voice in the shadows, "When I left you I was the apprentice, now I am the master,"

"Bzzzzzzz!" comes the reply.

"Oh for fuck's sake!" I whisper to myself.

K IS FOR...

KNOCK KNOCK & KINETICS

KNOCK KNOCK BY ANNA SKY

I mewled in frustration every time Matt touched my clit. It felt so swollen and sensitive and I was desperate for release. He let his fingers and tongue dance briefly against it, over and over, before moving on again. I thrust against him as best as my tethered wrists allowed but that only increased my frustration.

I thought my head would explode, I'd never felt like this before. Gone were the gentle strokes and slow romantic kisses which were nice enough but now I was into a whole new world. The scratching and grabbing until I wriggled in pain, combined with gentle circling motions, was a weird and heady mix.

"Please Matt," I begged. I was desperate, desperate enough to beg, something I thought I'd never do.

"Please Matt what?" he replied, circling his index finger over my clit. He knew what I wanted dammit, but he was determined to make things harder for me.

"I want to come, please let me come." My breathing came harder now, I was so close to the edge.

"Ask again," Matt said, still circling.

I nearly cried, this wasn't fair. I don't know how he got me wound up to this state but at that moment, I would have done anything he asked.

"Please let me come…." My voice trailed off; he was granting me my wish.

Matt slipped two fingers inside me, curving them up to stroke over and over. At the same time he brought his mouth to my clit and ran his tongue over the swollen surface. His other hand held me down by my stomach. No amount of bucking or writhing could get me my release; it all had to come from him.

He circled and sucked and with every movement I tried to push into him. The whole bed shook, the headboard banging against the wall in a continual 'knock knock' rhythm. And then finally he let me come, all the tension leaving my body in one massive surge.

It was a rush, and I felt myself pulsing hard round his fingers, I'd never come that hard before. I was light-headed, panting with effort and I closed my eyes to stop the sensory overload. It was like I was looking down on myself fractured into a thousand tiny pieces that were gradually building back into being me.

Slowly I came to. Matt was holding me tight again, stroking my hair and calling me a good girl. His words made no sense, but I felt safe and secure. Right now, that was enough for me.

KINETICS BY CHARLIE J FORREST

Begin Entry:
Subject: A.S.
Misdemeanour: Use of obscene language in public.
Punishment: Kinetics

Load Video: …
[video not available for this subject]
…
Load Audio: …
[audio not available for this subject]
…
Load kinaesthetic tactile reproduction:
Loading: Error
Loading: Error
Loading: Error
Diagnose Error: Insufficient security clearance to access this file.

Search all files: Files found
List files: Files found 'transcript'
Load transcript:
Loading:

Punishment Robot 12: You are subject A.S. correct?

Subject A.S.: Yes.

PR12: Confirm or deny.

AS: Confirm.

PR12: The sentence is kinetics. The volume is more than 12, less than 1,000

AS: Fewer

PR12: Rephrase statement.

AS: Clarification; correct term to use is fewer, not less.

PR12: Incorrect; punishment severity is deemed uncountable, therefore less.

AS: Question; but you said twelve, that makes it a–

PR12: –The sentence is kinetics. The volume is more than 24, less than 1,000.

AS: Hey, wait, that's not–

PR12: –The sentence is kinetics. The volume is more than 48, less than 1,000.

[INAUDIBLE]

PR12: Assume the position.

[SHUFFLING?]

PR12: Remove the trousers.

[INAUDIBLE]

PR12: Remove the… the undergarments.

AS: Really?

PR12: The sentence is ki–

AS: –Alright, alright, look they're gone!

PR12: You will say the words.

AS: I'm not saying them.

PR12: The sentence is kinetics. The volume is more than 96, less than 1,000.

AS: No, seriously, fuck off, I'm not saying the–

PR12: The sentence is kinetics. The volume is more than 192, less than 1,000.

AS: I'm not calling you that, you're a fucking robot!

PR12: The sentence is kinetics. The volume is more than 384, less than 1,000.

[INAUDIBLE]

[SOUND; PROBABLY STRIKE 1]

AS: One, thank you... sir.

L IS FOR...

LITTLE & LIPOSUCTION

LITTLE BY ANNA SKY

Matt released my arms from the headboard and I cuddled further into him. Tonight was a repeating cycle of pain or torment followed by comfort and hugs. It confused me but I hoped there was more to come. I'd experienced pain as pleasure for the first time, and had had the most intense orgasm of my life. All the while Matt cherished me, made me feel more loved than ever before.

Now as my brain and body relaxed, everything came into focus in my mind. I was Matt's for the night and all I had to do was trust him. I was normally fierce about my independence yet tonight I was happy for him to take charge. I giggled; it felt as though I were little all over again with no responsibilities, and I liked the feeling a lot.

"What're you laughing at?" Matt asked, still holding me tightly to him.

"I'm just happy," I replied and snuggled my head down harder against his chest.

"So am I," he said. "Why didn't we discover this side of ourselves years ago?"

"I don't know, hun…I know I wasn't brave enough to say anything." I waited for him to respond but he was quiet. My nerves made me fill in the silence. "I thought you'd run for the distant hills if I said I wanted you to spank me, I thought you'd think I was crazy."

"Oh no, little one." Matt replied. "I know you're crazy–"

I got my second wind and jumped on him, going straight for his ticklish spots. And then we were back in the cycle of him taking charge; he was on top of me pinning me down. A wicked glint in his eye told me I'd crossed some unspoken boundary and I wondered what else he had in store.

LIPOSUCTION BY CHARLIE J FORREST

I wanted it to end. No, that's not right; I wanted more than that, I wanted to go back to the beginning, to undo everything he'd done to me, to make it as if it had never happened.

So I made a list of everything I'd have to do, my own magical factory reset button. Liposuction; dentist; tattoo removal. Hiring men to take my belongings, throw away anything new, anything that wasn't there from the beginning. Hire a smart property lawyer to get me back into my old flat. Go through my phone and get in touch with everyone from a decade ago. Delete every photo, burn every letter.

Then what? Counselling? Therapy? Could I get a hypnotist perhaps, someone to make me forget all the hurt and the lies and the hour after hour of aching silence when all I wanted to do was cry?

But would that be enough?

Could I wrap myself back in my original packaging, slot myself back on the shelf, refold the box and pretend my warranty isn't void. Sit nice and pretty next to the new models, scuffed at the edges?

Except it wouldn't stop there. It would have to go deeper, take away the good too. The happy tears, the cuddles, the hot nights and the days that followed, where sitting was impossible and the memories incandescent. I'd have to get rid of the chair, the soft leather one that was the only thing I could bear to feel on my smarting backside the morning after, the same chair he'd sit on and have me kneel by his side. And the memory of every good thing, every kind word. Every pale line of healed flesh, ever judder of every aftershock of every single orgasm.

I wanted to hit the factory reset button, but I couldn't.

M IS FOR...

MÉNAGE & MUSHROOM

MÉNAGE BY ANNA SKY

Matt sat back on the bed, hands behind his head with his armpits showing; a typical alpha male pose. Except I'd never really seen him in it before – it just wasn't him. There was something different about him though. I couldn't quite put my finger on it, but looking at him, perhaps he sat just a little straighter. Maybe his shoulders were pushed back a bit more and his posture made him appear bigger. Whatever it was, it was damn sexy.

He grabbed one of my wrists and pulled me over to him. I groaned inwardly; I wasn't sure I could face going over his knee again.

"What's up, little one?" he asked, positioning me so I straddled his lap, facing him.

I said nothing, and lowered my lips tentatively to his. I wasn't sure whether making any first move was the right thing anymore. He had moaned at me in the past that he wanted me to be more assertive, but tonight, it didn't feel appropriate. Thankfully, he reciprocated. His lips were warm and soft, a direct contrast to when we'd arrived home earlier. He hands slid around my waist and I relaxed, this was like our lovemaking of old. Not the stale boring routine we'd fallen into, but a 'taking a break without taking our hands off each other' routine that we used to spend hours in. It was a sexy comfort blanket.

Matt slid his hands round, up and over my breasts. They looked small when cradled in his large hands and for a fleeting moment, I felt delicate and vulnerable again. My clit throbbed in response and I realised that he'd very much awoken something inside me. I wondered how we'd go forwards from this point; a decade of relationship irreversibly changed by a couple of hours. It sounded crazy.

Matt tweaked my nipples. "Earth to Fiona!"

"Ouch!" I replied, kissing him again and batted off his hands.

"What were you thinking?" He asked. "You looked so far away."

"Oh just that I've liked our little ménage à deux tonight so far," I smiled. "So, what other tricks have you got up your sleeve?"

MUSHROOM BY CHARLIE J FORREST

I would trust my black handled knife above any man. Passed breast to breast in the circle, charged with a thousand castings. It sits proud in my hand. I cannot tell if my hand has moulded to it or it to my hand.

The ground is thick with leaves, making movement difficult, every step, every crackling step is agonising, deafening. The leaf litter also hides my prey. Crouching low I scan back and forth for irregularities. Beneath a tree one of the brown sheets sits uncomfortably high. I flick it with the tip of my knife and cluck with pleasure at what it reveals.

My knife makes quick work of the mushrooms, slicing through the stalks like butter. I wrap them in paper and tuck the parcel into my bag.

"Stop right where you are!" comes a voice I don't recognise. I'd trust my knife above any man, right now I realise I can trust it above my own ears too. I slowly rise to my feet, turning to look in the direction of the voice.

He's a handsome sort, well dressed, but not too well dressed. Not one of the lord's family that's for sure. But certainly not one of the villagers either.

"What are you doing?"

I tug my forelock. "Nothing sir, just out for a walk in the woods and–"

"–What did you just put in your bag?"

I'm fucked and I know it. No sense in making matters worse. I toss open the flap of my bag and carefully withdraw the parcel. He holds out his hand and I place the bundle in it.

"Mushrooms?" he says, plucking one from within. I nod. "Well, it's not so bad as poaching I suppose. Very well, come here."

He perches himself on a tree stump a few feet away, brushing his coat aside and patting his knee invitingly.

I pause, unsure what he meant, I'm far too old to sit on a man's knee like a child. But then he grasps my wrist and flings me headlong over him. And, well, I guess I'm too old for what he does to me now. The indignity, the sheer humiliation of the act sets a fire of burning shame in my throat that leaves me unable to fight, face in the dirt, buttocks stinging from a vicious assault that I somehow can't believe is real.

When he tires he tosses me casually to the floor and, stooping, grabs my little bag of mushrooms. He holds one to his nose, sniffs. As he walks away I can hear the soft sounds of him chewing.

I pick up my bag and leave, chuckling under my breath. "There'll be one more at the Sabbat tonight I suppose" I whisper to the wind.

A CHEEKY REQUEST

INTERLUDE

We hope you're enjoying our stories so far. If you are, please consider leaving us an honest review.

Happy reviews give us the encouragement to keep writing and to get better at it.

And they make up for those really bad days when we'd rather be lion-tamers!

N IS FOR...

NOOOOOOOO! & NOROVIRUS

NOOOOOOOO! BY ANNA SKY

"Oh, I have a few tricks." Matt whispered in my ear. He trailed his fingertips from my cheek, over my lips and down over my throat. They paused in the hollow at the base of my neck as though waiting to feel a pulse. I breathed out, not realising that I'd been holding my breath in at all until then. Somehow, my brain told me the less I moved, the more I'd feel. His fingers danced lower, brushing over my breasts with the lightest of touches.

My body and brain were torn flickering between 'noooooooo! I couldn't possibly orgasm again!' and 'oh fuck me now, whatever you're doing is incredible'...My breathing came faster too, matching the rising excitement I felt running through me.

My skin felt electrified. It was sensitive but receptive to Matt's continued touch. I imagined little sparks from where his fingers connected with me, firing along neuron pathways and lighting me up. There were little flips of sensation in my belly and I felt my clit responding excitedly.

"You can't get enough of me, can you?" Matt whispered.

"No, I can't." I replied. "But it seems I'm not the only one that can't get enough."

Matt's fingers reached my pubis but skirted round and down to my inner thighs. I tried clamping my legs together to trap his hand where I wanted it to be, but failed. His fingers circled my inner thighs, and moved down to the backs of my knees before ending at my feet.

He massaged the soles of my feet, his thumbs stretching out my arches with firm strokes. It was heavenly, but not what I wanted right now. I wriggled impatiently. Matt rewarded me with a sharp tap to my leg.

"Just wait…good things come to those who wait, you know…"

NOROVIRUS BY CHARLIE J FORREST

It's easy to love someone on a sunny afternoon, with fresh-cut grass and lime tinted lager. Easy to love someone in the sweaty moonlight between crooner and saxophone solo. Love in moments like that means nothing.

"You look so fucking hot right now," he says.

"Don't be mean; I think I'm dying!"

I lift my head from the toilet bowl, he gently brushes some hair form my eye. For a moment our gazes meet. Then I feel something deep inside me and I don't know if it's a false alarm or not, but I take the safest option and return my head to where it was before.

"I think it's Ebola, or norovirus, or bubonic plague," I say.

He moves around behind me, his fingers slipping into the waistband of my jeans. I don't realise what he has planned until they slip around to the front. He pops open my button, teasing down my fly.

"What are you–?"

He silences me with a yank that drags my jeans to my knees, leaving me suddenly exposed. The air in the bathroom is cool against my skin. In spite of myself, and the awful juddering clenches that keep racking my body, a tiny bit of me doesn't want him to stop.

He nuzzles in close, his knees pushing mine further apart. He grasps a buttock in each meaty palm, pulling them gently aside. I feel something thick and warm and oh so deliciously hard resting between my parted cheeks. He leans over me, his cock rocking softly back and forth in the crease of my buttocks.

"I told you," he says, voice low, menacing, "you look so fucking hot right now!"

NOROVIRUS BY LOLA SPARKLES

I can't stand people who lie to me. To have had that little shit send me a text message, saying he couldn't make it this evening because he had norovirus? It was one lie too many!

I was going to make his miserable little arse pay. And the delightful thing was that once I started, he was going to love every minute. I was getting wet already, just at the thought of having him bent naked across my lap, the feel of his flaccid cock against my thigh.

Knowing that as he lay there, I would feel his cock grow with the anticipation of what was about to happen. I would run my hands delicately along his back, tracing a line down his spine to the top of his arse, before gently stroking each cheek.

Messing with his mind. The sensation of my hands and fingers tantalising him. Relaxing him before delivering the first smack. Waiting for him to say "One Mistress, thank you Mistress" before I would move on to the next. Delivering smack after smack with him thanking me after each one always had my pussy throbbing. Especially watching as his arse pinked up, and then turned red under my unforgiving ministrations.

Yes, that little shit was going to pay and he was going to thank me. And once I had delivered his punishment, I would be walking away, because no one lies to me.

O IS FOR...

ORCHESTRATED & OMNISCIENT

ORCHESTRATED BY ANNA SKY

It was a perfectly orchestrated finale. His ass was on fire, a criss-crossed mess of red welts and pink blushed highlights. He just needed the finishing blow. I brought my hand down sharply and enjoyed his body jerk in response, his hard cock trapped against my thighs.

I'd started with a low tempo, a slow warm up that gradually reddened his cheeks. He'd pushed up into my hand, welcoming the sensation. He'd stopped pushing when I increased the force behind each blow. It was only slight, but from his reaction I knew it had gone from pleasurable to crossing the threshold of pain.

He was my little pain whore though, the more pain I inflicted, the harder his prick got. I knew there would be a wet patch of pre-come on my thighs when we'd finished; he couldn't help himself. And I loved him for it, embracing his inner nature so readily.

Once I heard him breathing harder, managing my spanking, I increased the speed. He moaned, like the pain overflowed his body and out into the world. It was that noise right there that sang to me. That was the noise I longed for in any of our sessions, it was a primal response. Tonight I'd been feeling particularly evil and had felt him freeze when he heard me pull his belt out of its loops. He knew what that noise meant.

I had to control myself though. My boy could only take so much if I wanted to touch his delicious buttocks again in a week. And I had my own physicality to think of too, once the adrenaline wore off. My arm was currently on fire; all the muscles were hard and primed and my thighs were aching too. They'd supported his weight for the last half hour and it was time for him to thank me for it.

I dropped the belt and massaged his pain. I pushed it deep into his body, pressing and kneading until he was gasping and writhing under my hands. I rested one hand on his buttocks and slid the other up his back and into his hair.

"Good boy," I whispered, not knowing whether I was talking to me or him.

OMNISCIENT BY CHARLIE J FORREST

I call her goddess and people ask me why.

Why?

Like every other interaction I have needs to be pulled apart in this way. Why do I call you a friend, a lover a confidante?

I guess it's easier to explain why not; to nod my head and give them an answer, tacitly agreeing with their casual dismissal of cosa nostra; this thing of ours.

"No I don't literally worship her, at least not in that way," I say.

No I don't believe she has superhuman strength, or that if she wished she could part the sea.

Truth be told, I don't even believe she's the most divinely beautiful being on the planet. I wouldn't literally do anything for her. I don't truly believe I'm unworthy to even be in her presence.

But that's not the point.

A friend of mine, of the most eccentric variety, once summed it up brilliantly. He was talking about meta-religion; how people can worship fictional creations like Cthulhu or call themselves Jedi. In amongst the pretentious garbage about simulation versus simulacrum was one line that's always stuck with me:

"Don't treat these things as real, but do treat them as if they were real."

And, deep down, she knows this. When she catches my eye she can see the inner struggle, the insincerity, and the affection that comes with it. The fact that I will take reality and its imperfections and push through it for her. That's what really sets her apart, that's what would make me walk through fire for her.

Omniscient, divine, goddess.

P IS FOR...

PRESSED & PARAGON

PRESSED BY ANNA SKY

I was first pressed into service last night. It was an agonising wait; months from the facility through to being finally released. They bound me well for that time. I was wrapped tightly, unable to move, nothing to turn me on. My bed was comfortable though, a soft and fitted spot to lie and wonder what, or more accurately, who was to come.

Last night was the night. I was finally brought into the light, my bindings peeled off and my true form unveiled for the first time by someone who was going to love me, cherish me and make me buzz. They caressed me tenderly, appreciating my curves and squeezing just a little over my button. I'd been longing for that moment, I needed the pressure, needed the release. It was that little embrace that made me come alive.

After all that time alone, I didn't last long. I felt them fiddling behind me, and then they pushed something into my ass. I was affronted; surely they couldn't punish me for this? It wasn't my fault! There was a click and then I felt it, a jolt of pure energy running through my system. I was electrified, every cell stimulated. I quietly purred with joy, feeling a second wind. Treated right, I was going to go for hours, all that pent up energy that could be released.

And hell yeah baby, it was released! I buzzed, I whirled, I changed my rhythm. From a quiet hum all the way to the biggest roar, I was the centre of her universe. When she came, she contracted so hard around me, I thought I was going to burst. I was her new best friend.

PARAGON BY CHARLIE J FORREST

This guy, this fucking guy!

Life used to be nice and straightforward. Nice and simple. I had this easy way of living, where I knew what I wanted. Where everything that I went after I got. People would worship me, dropping to their knees at a glance, offering their wrists and throats and hearts. And I was gracious in my divinity, taking them, raising them up for a time, bringing them into paradise by casting them into inferno.

But then, there was this guy y'know. He wasn't like the others. I mean, that didn't stop me treating him like the rest. Fool that I was, where divine right failed I tried violence and bluster.

He laughed. Laughed and took my hand. He took my hand. HE took MY hand. It was impertinent, it was sacrilege. And what's more I let him do it. I let HIM, or at least that's what I told myself, that's what I whispered over and over to myself, my own little mantra, my litany of lust.

It couldn't last. I couldn't last. I saw it in the eyes of the others.

"You've changed," I could hear them whisper. "You're not who you were. You're tainted, weak, one of us!"

So I sent him away. Sent him away and burned every inch of the bridge that had formed between us. But it was too late. Yes the others were there as before, and maybe those whispers were just in my head. But it was a pale imitation. As a beat my hand sore and leant close, milking every ounce of their cries into my ears, all I could feel was jealousy.

He ruined me, spoiled me for everyone else. This guy, this fucking guy, my paragon of perversion.

PRESSED BY LOLA SPARKLES

"You just know that it would be awesome though…"
"What would be awesome?"
"Sex with him…"

"Please tell me you're not saying what I think you're saying?"

"Why on earth not?"

"Well, don't the tights put you off?"

"They are not tights!"

"Yes they are."

"No they're not, they're breeches."

"They look like tights."

"Well they are not tights, they are super-hot tight trousers, and well just look at the boots…"

"You're seriously worrying me now and destroying one of my all-time favourite movies…"

"He is the reason it is my favourite movie, just look at the hair and the outfit and at the end when he is doing the thing on the stairs….and WOW that is now making me want to do kinky things on the stairs with him."

"Lola you are seriously screwed in the head…"

"No I'm not, just his whole persona, domineering, controlling he wants to own her and control her…and seriously if it was me, screw the baby!"

"You are desecrating my childhood memories. I need more wine to be able to deal with this level of crazy."

"In the scene in the ballroom I can just imagine being pressed against his chest as he waltzes me between the other dancers. Oh and don't even get me started on how hot I find the whole masked ball."

"If I had known watching your favourite childhood movie was going to lead to this I would have declined the invitation!"

"I just know that if it was me and him in a room that he would get me, understand me. Bending me to his will, owning and worshipping my body. After all that is what he is offering to her."

"I really do not need the mental pictures you are painting in my head!"

"I haven't even started on how I can imagine him taking my arms, grasping them behind my back as he rips my blouse from my body, pulling me against his chest, slowly stroking my cheek before his fingertips trail down to my breast…"

"STOP! Just stop please, I don't want to hear any more of your strange fantasies about the king of the goblins"

"It's Goblin King actually…"

Q IS FOR...

QUIM & QUINCE

QUIM BY ANNA SKY

Quinella Ursula Imogen Markham. Yeah, what initials did your parents land you with? Mine landed me with the worst of all…fucking QUIM. Of all the names in the world, that was the one that would ensure I'd be bullied, side-lined and generally have the piss taken out of me for. Sticks and stones will break my bones but words will never hurt me…oh yeah? Whoever wrote that was never surrounded in the playground and called all names under the sun. By the time I left school they called me "the big C"…all done in jest but every time they called me that, whether you thought of it as cancer or cunt, it cut straight to my core. Children are vicious.

But it taught me adults can be vicious too, and now they pay me to be. I'm Mistress Q. Risen from the ashes, a phoenix to their flame. I know their darkest desires, understand their perversions. I'm the one they turn to, wanting absolution for their sins. Instead of taunting me, they're begging me, begging me for mercy. I'm the only one that grant them that. And I don't take my position lightly. They have to earn their forgiveness.

It's not easy; they have to prove they're worthy. They have to crawl and grovel, tell me their darkest secrets. They have to let me hurt and rebuild them. And if they're worthy, if they are truly worthy, I will grant them that. I will release them from their servitude to me, and let them out into the world. They'll be better for it, and never fucking call someone quim again.

QUINCE BY CHARLIE J FORREST

An arm appears across my chest. I scarcely have time to register it before I'm pulled back against him. He drags my arms behind my back, the rope snaking around my wrists. He traces a hand up my back. Brushing against the back of my neck. Then his grip is on my forehead, pulling my head back into him as he wraps the lines across my face, covering my eyes, pulling my hair into a dishevelled mess, like a four year old wrapping a birthday present.

He pushes me to my knees, arms wrapping tight around me as he lowers me onto my side, then onto my front. The rope gives me just enough slack to make my wrists comfortable, but only just.

I can't see, but I know he's watching me, eyes running over my bare skin, the primitive, lustful part of his brain picking what to do next.

He grabs my hips, pulling me up to meet him, but instead if just taking me, pressing his cock against my opening, he pauses. I shiver a little as he applies cool lube to me, carefully coating my entrance ready for–what?

What?

Oh sweet Jesus fuck, what is that!?!

Ten minutes of spluttering ecstatic agony later he wraps himself around me like a second skin, a living bandage to kiss away my hurts.

"What... What was that...before?" I ask.

"Quince," he mumbles, shuffling a yawn.

"A what?"

"A quince. I bought it down at the farmers market."

My mind races.

"No," I say, "a quince isn't like a fruit, it's a thing in physics."

"Is it?"

"Yeah like a unit for magnetic radiation or something."

"Are you sure?"

"Yeah, either that or it's a regional capital of somewhere on the India Bangladesh border?"

"Then what the hell is this?" he asks, pulling an object out from the tousled bedsheets.

I look at him, long and hard, trying to force him into laughing first.

"That," I say, "is a pineapple!"

QUIM BY LOLA SPARKLES

She said she wanted to be a writer. She wanted to write about the hot passionate nights we had. She wanted to write stories that would have people reaching down to stroke their cocks or tease their clits.

She wanted to write about our life, worship me in words. Use me, her Domme, as her muse and our relationship as her inspiration. I consented especially as she had begged so prettily to be allowed; she'd chosen her moment so carefully. Her face covered in my juices, her eyes gazing up at me, glazed with lust, following a particularly intense scene. Knowing that this was my weakest moment, the moment where I would give her the moon if I could; she'd asked and I'd said yes.

My only rule about her writing was that she had to get over her aversion to the word cunt. I did not want to see any of the normal namby–pamby shit she would normally use to describe that most beautiful treasure of hers, written down. Yoni, pussy, vajajay...none of those really conveyed the raw sexuality of our time together, and therefore would not do for the stories she wanted to weave.

Today she emailed me to say that her first story had gone live. She was so excited and her enthusiasm was infectious. I was delighted for her and said that she could have a very special reward this evening. She sent the link and as I read her story, all thoughts of rewarding her left my mind. The little bitch had deliberately disobeyed me.

Instead of recognising and owning the beauty of the word cunt, she'd chickened out and let her aversion to the word take over. Not only that, she hadn't even replaced it subtly or chosen a word that would continue the flow of the story. No she had gone with my most hated word for cunt...quim.

R IS FOR...

RESOURCEFUL & RA-RA SKIRT

RESOURCEFUL BY ANNA SKY

I loved the way he handled the sausages; I could watch him for hours. It was his deft fingers and nicely proportioned wrists. And the look of concentration on his face as he so accurately sliced to his customer's demands.

I stared from the safety of the cheese counter opposite. Occasionally he'd catch my eye and wink, dazzling me with a cheeky grin and I'd smile back briefly before looking away, embarrassed by his overt gestures. What if he knew what I was thinking?

I wanted him to run his hands over me, handling me like one of his chunks of meat. Firm and precise, resourceful in his movements. I wanted him to test and squeeze, and hold me down like one of his salamis.

When they moved us both to the bakery it was nearly my undoing. I watched him prepare the dough, kneading and squeezing. He'd slam the mixture onto the work bench and the air left my lungs, as though I were the dough itself.

His fingers were so deft and nimble when he prepared the pastries. He'd frown slightly as he made each one a perfect replica of the last. He'd tweak and pinch, ensuring perfection. My nipples hardened at the mere thought of him making the pain au chocolats.

But it was the bread preparation that I felt most viscerally. I wanted him to grip me hard enough to leave imprints of his fingers on my breasts, my stomach, my thighs. I wanted him to slap and knead at my flesh until I could take no more, that he'd knocked all the air out of me. And then like the dough, I'd rise again, triumphantly.

RA-RA SKIRT BY CHARLIE J FORREST

"What the fuck is this?" I asked.

"It's a skirt."

"What, no. What you're wearing is a skirt this is a… a… circus costume. I mean what the hell are these bits. You can't seriously be asking me to wear this?"

"I'm not asking," she said.

The words send my gut twisting and I'm at once horny and frightened, startled more by how much power she has over me than what it is she's actually asking, no, telling me to do.

The queue for the club is long, and cold. The rain just about holds off, but given the time of year it's still enough to leave me quivering all over in the worst possible way.

When we get inside it all gets worse. Friends, acquaintances, ex-lovers. They all spot me at once and even though I stare at the floor giving my best 'fuck the fuck off!' pose they still insist on bounding over, saying hello to her and telling me how good I look. How it's great to see me broadening my horizons, about how fucking cute the skirt blancmange thing looks on me. My cheeks burn, I want to curl into a ball and claw my way into the ground, or punch everyone and everything in the face. My cheeks are twin volcanoes of shame.

I want to cry.

The realisation hits me hard. It's the one thing I've never done for her; the one frontier that we skirted so very, very close to but never quite reached. And now here I am and she's going to make me do it in front of everyone.

I want to leave. I decide to leave. I slip away from her while she's talking to someone, make it to the cloakroom and spend ten minutes hovering next to the door attracting weird looks from the bouncers. Then I go back, hurl my coat at the cloakroom attendant, and sneer at the barman as I get the drink I'd mumbled about when I slipped away. And I go back to her.

She knows, of course she knows. I've never been much good at lying. But she doesn't say anything, just picks up where we left off. And that's it, no punishment, no chastisement. After a while the anger settles, sinking into my boots and taking something with it, a weight I didn't know I'd been carrying.

Later on, when we're curled up in the back of a taxi, she says, "I know that was hard for you." I make non-committal grunts and she goes on. "It was lovely to see you working through that. Even though you hated it, seeing you do that for me. I'm very proud of you right now."

And that's when I gave her my tears.

S IS FOR...

SILENT & SANDPAPER

SILENT BY ANNA SKY

I laid there, absolutely silent. I had to be; the gag was fitted tightly in my mouth, and if I made even the slightest noise, the merest whisper of a sound he would switch from the small wooden cane to one of two things. Either the wooden hair brush which hurt like fuck, or the white plastic cane which hurt like fuck. A horrible choice. I hated both these implements and never wanted him to use either one. He delighted in my pain and torment, and the more I hated what he did, the harder he was.

I couldn't move my arms or legs. I was tied face down, spread-eagled on the bed, rope pulling tightly from all four limbs to the bed posts. My joints were stretched so I couldn't wriggle or move; I had to take what he inflicted.

He counted the strokes with the cane, we were up to twenty and my arse felt like it was on fire. Every strike was accompanied by his hand exploring the new mark that had angrily bloomed on my skin. He cooed in glee at every sandwiched welt of red, white, red and massaged it hard into my flesh with his fingers. They grabbed and pinched and made me want to whimper. I didn't dare.

He tormented me with names, telling me who and what I really was. The words tripped off his tongue, so coarse yet true. I nearly came from hearing him recognise my true self alone; the physical pain was just a bonus. I was in heaven.

SANDPAPER BY CHARLIE J FORREST

When he has me tied and blindfolded he can do anything. And he knows it too. He likes to take away my control, have me fastened down good and tight. I love that feeling, that complete immobility. It's like there are two warring feelings going on. There's the me that lives inside my head that just wants to drift away and leave my body behind like a hermit crab's shell. I swear if he did that and just left me I'd sleep like a baby. Well, maybe not like a bay, but I would be gone, oblivious to my bare skin, spread legs and the small perforated ball-gag resting between my jaws.

But then he begins and the other me takes over. The me that is completely there and in the moment, that makes my legs quiver in anticipation, makes the wood of the chair creak as I strain against my bonds. The first time he was so nice to me. My skin was treated to soft tickling feather strokes, and smooth warm caresses. The second time these were mixed with the tingle of ice-cubes and the scrape of his nails down my back. He must have known he had me by the long juddering moans he was able to draw from my throat.

Then came other sensations, the pegs or clamps or whatever it is that he uses to crush my nipples into tight buds of agony, the cool sharp metal that spells out words on my thighs, words that make me want to blush and come all at once.

But tonight, tonight he's got something new.

He places his hand firm against my back. I can feel there's something wrong, something cool and harsh. But it's only when he starts to move that I recognise the touch of the sandpaper. My jaw drops so far the gag almost comes free and even though I can't see a thing, deep down I know, I just know that the noise I make leaves him grinning.

T IS FOR...

TREMBLING & TURTLE

TREMBLING BY ANNA SKY

She stood, trembling. He was here, the one she revered above all others. She would follow him to the ends of the Earth and back, which wasn't hard as he left a distinct trail. He was the Great Slugliness, Master of "Things That Go Bump in the Night". Or rather, in his case, tapping.

For he loved tap dancing; nothing made him happier, or his observers more covered in slime. The scent of his trail would pull in his followers for miles around, it would put their pheromone-detection on high alert. Men would leave their wives for that smell alone. Women would almost orgasm at the merest whiff.

And when everyone converged to see the Lord of the Dance, miraculous and sexual things would happen. First, there'd be adulation. And everyone getting their groove on. The more slime, the fewer the clothes being worn. It brought out everyone's inner sexy beast, the slime felt so damn good. Like sparks flying, hundreds of tiny digits squeezing and pinching and stroking.

Yet after a while that still wasn't enough. Everyone wanted more. There was no relief from the sexual tension the slime provoked. The second phase was the orgy phase. Bodies all over, wrapping round each other and sliding in the mucousy mire. Tongues and teeth, fingers and phalluses. The licking of labia, caressing of clits, pulling of pricks until everyone merged into one massive gooey continuum.

And there was always the chosen one. The one who could stand there and wait for His attention, who wouldn't be affected by the urgent need to frig and fap and moan as they hit the big O, over and over.

They would be invited to dance and if they could keep up with the slug, tap to his rhythm until he was sated, they would transcend all the others. They'd be taken to the highest of highs and plied with his special stash of slime until they begged for mercy. Tonight, it would be her.

TURTLE BY CHARLIE J FORREST

"So which one was your favourite then?"

"Leonardo," says Mike.

"Michelangelo," says John.

"Wait," I say, "seriously? Could you two be more predictable?"

"But look, Leonardo was the leader, therefore the best, QED."

"Yeah but Michelangelo was the cool one–"

"–no, he was the stupid one. The one that was the butt of all the jokes."

"No he wasn't, that was the reporter."

"April?"

"No, not April, the guy she had to work with, the one with the braces and long hair and the stupid accent. Michelangelo was the rebel. And he had the coolest weapon."

"Now you're just wrong there, everyone knows sword beats nunchucks hands down."

"Tell that to Bruce Lee."

I put my face in my hands and let out a low groan of disappointment. It cuts the pair of them short and they glare at me.

"So predictable," I say shaking my head. "All you guys ever think of is the violence, never the important stuff."

"Well, no, there's more to it than– okay what's your favourite?"

"Splinter," says John.

"Better fucking not be, Christ, that's like saying you've got a thing for older guys and being condescend…"

My look cuts the words down in his throat.

"Actually it's Donatello," I say.

"What? But he's the loser," says John.

"No he's not."

"Yeah," says Mike, "He's right. I mean in any group of characters there's one designated loser. I mean the one that gets all the shit attributes. And that's Donatello right there. I mean look at him, nerdy, quiet, whiny and with the worst fucking weapon."

"You're wrong," I whisper. I can feel their eyes burning into me and I cup my pint, staring into the amber liquid as I lay it out for them.

"He's not just quiet, he's thoughtful. He's the only one of the group that would rather solve a problem by thinking than just doing stuff. Ok, I mean I know there's something to be said for bravery and leadership, but half of leadership is knowing that you don't know everything and being able to draw on the skills of those on your side. And his weapon isn't the worst. It's one that says a lot about him. You know Buddhist monks? Well they used to carry staffs like that. They were banned from carrying weapons so they pretended that they were just ornamental, for warding off bad spirits. But in reality they could use them as well as any sword if they needed to. I mean yes they're probably not the best thing to charge into battle with, but that's not who he is. He's the thoughtful one, the one who will use force if there is no other way but does so reluctantly. A sword kills, but a stick is different, a stick can stop a fight without blood… That's who he is, one who will hurt you but only to guide you onto the right path."

I let my eyes slowly trace their way up from the table. They're watching me with rapt awe.

"You... you actually manage to make him sound kind of sexy," John says. I nod and offer my hand for a hi-five.

"Turtle Power," we whisper.

U IS FOR...

UNDERGROUND & UGANDA

UNDERGROUND BY ANNA SKY

Anna's note: SORRY SORRY SORRY, but it forced its way out of my head...

When the Slug King finds his chosen one, he stops dancing for a few seconds. Instead, he slips in his slime and causes a wave of ecstasy running through the horny crowd, starting with whoever he comes into contact with. He shimmies, and shakes his ass and the chosen one responds in kind. It's a mating ritual, an unspoken game. They, for the Slug King is truly pansexual, approach His Slugliness. Carefully, for lack of grip in the exudate underfoot.

And once there, they embrace. The chosen one rubbing their body against that of the slug. Slipping and sliding and coating themselves in his generous gloop, leaving no skin un-gooed. Together they will slide off, leaving the heaving horny masses to their masturbation and orgy-fuelled orgasms.

Together they twist and turn until they reach the secret underground lair of the great Slug King. There they fall into a sticky embrace, the slime gluing them together. Now there is no escape for the Chosen One. They have to submit, allow the Slug King to devour and dine upon their sexual prowess. He teases with his radula, ghosting his denticles along every sensitive inch of flesh.

He loves the taste of fresh arousal, the heady scent of edging towards orgasm. Whether cock or cunt he loves the juices, the breathless need for him. He licks and slurps and releases his finest slime. It's what they've been waiting for. The elixir of the slime God.

And when orgasm comes for the Chosen One, they transcend the highest of highs, reach an immortal high and spread their wings. His Slugliness ensures that they don't fall like Icarus and as they fly, masturbates furiously until he encloses them both in a safe sac of thick gunge until morning comes.

UGANDA BY CHARLIE J FORREST

There are problems with having a crush on a colleague. And I mean aside from the obvious harassment, gross misconduct and stationery cupboard issues. The main one being that it makes it just that little bit harder to tell if she's making a move on you.

She travels for work. I get that. And yes it was expected for a partner to take an associate under their wing to get some first-hand experience of international law. So when she asked me to shadow her on this trip then it was completely above board.

And she used her air miles to bump me up to premium executive so we could work on the flight also made perfect sense.

So did the shared taxi, hotel suite and the dinner together in the restaurant. It all made sense, it all felt so right, so natural. And when we got into the lift and I felt her hand in mine it just felt right. It felt right all the way down the corridor, through the door and onto the sofa. Her hand on my cheek, her lips brushing against mine. It was more than I ever could have hoped for and I hated myself for interrupting what was turning into the best evening of my life but an image from a CNN documentary suddenly filled my head.

"Wait," I said, "I don't understand."

She pulled away like I'd slapped her and I quickly reached out, drawing her back to me.

"No it's not that it's just. Why here? Why Uganda? I mean you know what they do to... to..."

She kissed me again then sat up, pulling me awkwardly upright with her.

"It's the reason I do what I do. Because the fight's not over yet. When this is all over we can go back to our home and not have to worry. We can march and sing and have a party. But here, a couple of years ago they were arranging their first pride march. They knew it was illegal, that bad things would happen if they were caught. But the crazy fuckers did it anyway and. I don't know, I kind of wanted to share that feeling and... fuck! I really do suck at seduction."

I shook my head and tried to silence her with my lips.

"Crazy fuckers?" I thought, "I think I like the sound of that."

V IS FOR...

VIPERA BERUS & VOLVO

VIPERA BERUS BY ANNA SKY

The club was hot and sticky, the air con long gone. It wasn't the sort of place you'd choose to visit unless you lived in town, where it was about the only entertainment going. The place stunk of sweat and beer, cigarette stubs lined the floor. It was a classy dive.

I was an out-of-towner, stuck in this hell hole for the next few days, chasing contracts for my employer. All I wanted was an ice-cold beer and this is where the motel had sent me. I stuck out like a sore thumb; I wasn't exactly attired for the climate in my suit and shirt. My tie had long been jettisoned and the shirt was unbuttoned as far as was decent.

I rubbed my eyes. They were sore in the dry air and I wasn't even sure how far I could see straight. It was then the music started. The room fell silent, everyone turned to face the makeshift stage. I heard a whisper "Vipera

Berus" in a hushed voice. I frowned to myself – it sounded like some kind of snake?

A woman strode out, her clothing left little to the imagination. She positioned herself against the pole at stage centre. The beat changed then, a faster tempo and she began to writhe. She was long-limbed and flexible and wove her way around in sleek twisting movements. A sheen of sweat reflected off her making it difficult to focus on her in the dim lighting and with my tired eyes.

She had a tattoo winding from her thigh, up round her torso and between her breasts. As she danced in fluid, languid movements, I could have sworn the damn thing moved. I blinked. It had to have done; now its tail was between her legs, its face meeting her lips as she parted them in ecstasy.

I blinked again, fuck I was tired. The tattoo was back where it started. The woman looked at me and winked and blow me, if the damn snake didn't do the same. Time to get out of freaky town…

VOLVO BY CHARLIE J FORREST

"It'll be fun."

"For you maybe," I said.

"Ah come on, where's your sense of adventure?"

"Adventure is one thing, this is just indecent exposure and a shortcut to a criminal record."

He rolled his eyes at me and pulled open the door of the old Volvo, beckoning me into the passenger seat.

He slammed it with the kind of dull thud you can only manage on cars of a certain age, the dull, firm clunk of heavy metal and thick sun-bleached plastic.

He climbed into the driver's seat, started the car and we were off.

Lindisfarne is in the far north, several hours' drive even from my little place in the countryside.

He drives, I gaze out of the rain streaked window, glad of the warm stream of air from the heater. As we pull onto the motorway I give up pretending to be awake and let the thrum of the car tyres carry me off into a doze.

I wake up uncomfortable, my skin prickling. Sweat drips down my cheek. The seat beneath me is impossibly hot.

"You know what I love about these old Scandinavian cars?" he asks.

"Ugh, hmm, whassmattter? Too– ugh," I manage.

"It's the fact they all come with heated seats as standard, you know, for the cold Nordic winters."

I blink, realise my hand is feebly pawing at my t-shirt, skin damp with sweat, buttocks aflame.

"Stop it," I say, "turn the heater off!"

He looks at me, just for a moment before turning his eyes back to the road. The bastard said nothing, just grinned that stupid smug fucking grin.

I reached for the controls for the heater. The first time, he lands a stinging blow on the back of my hand. I pull it back, cradling it against my chest and trying to quell my racing heart. A minute or two later I try again. This time his fingers wrap tight around my wrist and I can feel in the way he holds me, his strength tempered, using just enough to put me in my place.

"No," he says, "you know what you can do if you're feeling hot."

He lets go.

I shuffle in the seat, made uncomfortable by more than the heat from the vents.

I stare furiously out the windscreen, not catching his eye. The wipers smear the real world into focus with a regular beat as I wriggle against the bonds of the seatbelt, peeling the clothes from my flushing skin.

W IS FOR...

WATCHERS & WART

WATCHERS BY ANNA SKY

Strapped to the St Andrew's cross in the centre of the floor, I closed my eyes to reduce the visual overload. The noises didn't diminish though. The whoosh and the crack of a whip sounded somewhere to my left, the staccato crackle of a violet wand behind me and the regular smack of someone receiving a good hard spanking. I felt the buzz in my head, my limbs soften, vague euphoria beckoning. This is where I belonged, in my subspace.

Whispers immediately behind me drew me back to the present. I wondered what they were planning. A grand display for the watchers? Double handed flogging, wrists whirling to keep the tails spinning, constantly biting into my flesh? Or maybe the cane, tap-tap-tapping its way over my buttocks, me trying not to clench as it struck?

I imagined hundreds of eyes on me as I was punished, I felt them bore into my back. I couldn't see who was actually there, but the idea of anonymous observers excited me. Perhaps they would murmur amongst themselves, rate the way I took the pain. Maybe they'd criticise me, call me degrading names. My pulse raced at the thought.

Or maybe they'd stand in silence, each lost to their own bubble of ecstasy, getting off on my pain. Hands would reach into clothing, freeing dewy-tipped dicks, or relieving pent-up pressure on swollen clits.

I no longer knew whether being shackled to the cross was about me, or them. Was it for my pain or their pleasure? My head buzzed; this is where I belonged, in my subspace.

WART BY CHARLIE J FORREST

He passes me his phone, not wanting to say it out loud.

"Wart?" I splutter.

"Yes," he says, reaching forward and swiftly tugging his phone free from the eruption of half swallowed tea. "Except it's pronounced like art."

"Wart?" I say, rolling the unfamiliar word around my mouth. "Why does your mother call you that?"

"Well my full name's Arthur, and mum was a bit of a literary freak."

I look at him blankly.

"Wart? T.H. White? Once and Future King?" he says.

I sweep a hand across my face and back over my head.

"It was the nickname King Arthur had when he was a boy."

"Oh," I say. "You know you might want to lead with that first next time."

"Why?"

"Well, because it might lead to... assumptions."

"What? About warts you mean?"

I glance around on the off chance that there's anyone in the coffee shop that hasn't heard our conversation.

"Yes," I hiss.

"But you can see I'm not warty."

"Not on your face maybe, but she is your mother... she's seen things I haven't."

"Well what difference does that make to anyone?"

I prop my head on my fist and look at him.

"Anyone?" I say.

I can watch the thoughts telegraphing his face: puzzlement, suspicion, realisation, awkward stunned silence.

"Come on," I say reaching over and taking his hand. "I'm very nearly a doctor and I think you might be in need of a very thorough examination."

X IS FOR...

MARKS THE SPOT & XENOPLASTIC

MARKS THE SPOT BY ANNA SKY

My eyes were tightly screwed shut...there was no way I was going to watch *this*. A light tap on my tragus was enough to make my whole body clench.

"Relax," a voice said. "It was just a marker pen."

Despite myself, I had to ask. "What for?"

"I draw an X – marks the spot I'm going to pierce."

I tensed again; it meant the next touch was going to hurt like a bitch. I took in a deep breath, perhaps I wouldn't feel the pain as much and I'd be still, rather than breathing and perhaps it wasn't too late to change...oh fuck!

Breathe out, breathe the pain out...

I cracked my eyes open. Big mistake – there was a long needle type thing *poking out of the side of my head*.

I winced as it moved. It wasn't a dull throb, just sharp wincing agony.

"Nearly there." The labret was being fixed in place, a trophy of bravery to display to the world.

Those final few seconds were almost nauseating. The room span, my head span and a sheen of sweat beaded on my forehead. I sat absolutely still in the chair, the pain already transforming into something else until I was horny as hell. The endorphins kicked in and I flew.

My eyes still closed, I felt lips pressing to my own, the chair moving as thighs straddled themselves over my legs. Hands bearing down on my shoulders, pinning me in place. I left my mind to process the pain, let my body respond to the stimuli, bucking up, hips thrusting as best I could.

I kept my eyes shut, enjoying the ride.

XENOPLASTIC BY CHARLIE J FORREST

"Do you have protection?"

"From what? Oh, you mean... do people still call it that?"

"Yes."

"Isn't it a little, you know, old fashioned?"

She cocks an eyebrow at me and I know I've got it wrong again.

"Not old fashioned?" I ask. She shakes her head. "Still physical device?" I ask. She nods her head.

"You know how you said it might be a bit weird, is this what you meant?"

"No, I mean I can see that, yes. That last bit was a bit weird, but that's not the weird bit."

She folds her arms over her breasts and I start to wonder whether I shouldn't have just kept my mouth shut.

"There's a weirder bit?"

"Ummm, kind of," I say. She rolls her eyes. Brilliant white against her dusky skin.

"Go on then," she says, "let's see if the novelty of shagging a bloke with a time machine is worth the aggro."

"Well, you see, I haven't always been off gallivanting. There was a while, a good long while, where I had just had enough. So I went off somewhere a little more laid back."

"Victorian era?"

"What? No! What makes you say that?"

"Thought it might explain the facial hair."

I run a finger self-consciously over the glorious soft plumage of my moustache, but press on.

"Actually it was the Neolithic- don't look at me like that. I was, looking for somewhere quiet and, well, it doesn't get much quieter than that."

"Anyway, I fell in with a lovely group living somewhere in what I think would become Somerset. We had a lot of adventures; hunting mammoths, eating mammoths, making hand axes and spears ready for hunting mammoths."

"So, pretty mammoth heavy schedule then?"

"Well it wasn't just mammoth hunting you know. Especially when the sun goes down and you're huddling around the campfire, arm in arm, hand in loincloth so to speak. But that's sort of where the weird bit comes in."

"Genetics, you see, can be a bit fiddly. On a long enough timescale it becomes a bit... well. You know when you're trying to peel sellotape and it rips, and the bit you pull either comes off completely or takes over the while roll? Well it's a bit like that."

She stares at me blankly.

"Are you saying you're turned on by sticky tape? Because I can probably be on board with that."

"No, it's not that it's, I, umm. Look, over a long enough time scale you either become a common ancestor to everyone on the planet or to nobody... And I don't know which is the case."

"Wait, so if we fuck that might make it incest?"

"Well not incest exactly. You see it'd only be very distant and it's more xenoplastic than incestuous and–"

I'm cut short by her finger pressing against my lips.

"Does that mean I have to call you 'Daddy'?"

"Err, no..."

"Can I do it anyway?"

I'd forgotten how much I live 21st century women.

Y IS FOR...

YODELLING & YIDDISH

YODELLING BY ANNA SKY

High on the hilltop I stood in the breeze. I'd not seen a soul for days, just the way I like it. At this altitude it was still warm but exposed, and I made the most of it, letting the sun hit as much of my skin as possible at any one time. I'd found my favourite spot, a flat slab worn smooth over millennia and it was here I spent my time. A small pack of provisions kept me throughout the day and I lay, the rock supporting my back, warming my bones as I let my mind wander. The sun streamed down on my naked front, warming my thighs and belly, and deliciously heating my more tender spots.

The first few days I didn't dare try what I wanted to; but now I was happily into my groove, letting my voice carry across the valley, echoing around and being absorbed by the trees. When I finally got it right, the yodelling was an intense experience. The low pitched rumbling in my chest contrasted with the high buzzing that my falsetto created. My voice leapt dramatically between octaves and as it did so, I realised that I felt alive, free and deeply sensual.

I practised more and more, the vibrations running through me made my nipples taught, caused my abdominal muscles to clench in anticipation and set my sexual energy alight. After each session I'd settle back onto my rock and slowly let my fingers roam, finding my sweet spots until I roared to a climax, the yodels still echoing in my head.

YIDDISH BY CHARLIE J FORREST

He hates boring words. He says it's something to do with the "Standard Narrative" that he doesn't like the idea that some words can't just be what they are, they're different.

Proxies I guess, place markers. Love doesn't mean love. If it did we would use it so much more. But we don't because we're scared of the thing that society has turned it into.

"I love you," isn't just that feeling, it's something bigger, too big. A declaration of insurmountable feelings. A lifelong commitment and something that you're not allowed to not reciprocate. Because it's the ultimate; love me or get the fuck out of my life.

He hates that. Hates the word hate. So instead he whispers words I don't always understand. He recites German poetry as we walk through the park. He tells vulgar jokes in Greek. And when we're alone he leans in close and mutters dirty words in Yiddish. He says he's describing what he's about to do with me and every time I listen desperately for some clue. And every time it's lost on me and all I can do is put my body in his hands as he pulls implements from the wall, letting out cries of delight as he puts them to use on me. Cries in Russian, or perhaps Polish, mutterings in Italian, Korean, Danish and Scouse. Ah what the fuck do I care, it's all Portuguese to me.

YIDDISH BY LOLA SPARKLES

"Our grandmother used to love to drop the odd Yiddish word into conversation…"

I could hear my sister in the background reading the eulogy she had prepared for our grandmother's funeral. The congregation around me were in varying states of mourning but all I could do was smile to myself remembering the silliness and fun my gran had exuded with every breath.

Yes she had indeed dropped the odd Yiddish word into conversation, especially with her non Jewish friends where she would use words such as *farshtelnik* and everyone would think she was saying something really honourable. When actually she was just dropping in the word for drag queen and seeing whether she could get away with it.

I could feel myself chuckling at the mere memory of her mirth the first time she had done it, as I tried to not obviously giggle I looked up and caught the eye of the celebrant. He had a twinkle in his eye and I could see that he was wondering as to why I was smiling on this day of sadness. What he didn't know is that I could just imagine my gran's response to him, he was stunning and she would not have been afraid to tell him that he was a hunk, she would have probably followed it with something along the lines of if I was only 50 years younger.

I looked up and caught his eye again, maybe I should go over and tell him that I thought he was a hunk, after all I was 50 years younger and there was a lot I could imagine doing with him.

Z IS FOR...

ZENITH & ZOOCHOROUS

ZENITH BY ANNA SKY

The earth was cold and damp on my back, moulding round my shoulders. I welcomed its soft support. Up above my head, far up into the zenith, stars twinkled. The light of distant places, probably already dead, disappeared into the dark unwelcoming void of the universe. No-one would mourn their loss; no-one would miss an individual dazzling presence. Just one star didn't make a difference right now.

I came back down to earth, grounded by the heaving lump on top of me. I shouldn't have done it really, but that's what grief can do; get you blind drunk and agree to a stupid shag with the guy that really liked you from afar for too many years. He wasn't bad looking, was quite pleasant really, but we'd never got past the small talk.

When he took me by the hand earlier, and led me behind the outhouse, I'd not argued. And when he slipped his hand inside my blouse, I'd leant into him, wordless encouragement. He kissed me on my neck. Circled his thumbs around the hard nubs of my nipples. He did everything right and in my emptiness, I let the 'sex by numbers' happen. I wanted to feel something, feel more than the void but he couldn't fill it, couldn't empty me of grief.

I shouldn't have let it happen, but even when I heard the rip of the condom packet, I didn't care. I spread my legs when he wanted me to, let him press insistently against me until my body relented. It didn't take him long; he was full of blustering apology but I assured him it didn't matter. It really didn't.

He sorted himself out and in the only gesture that nearly cracked my silent veneer, handed me a tissue for me to clean up with. It's the little things that can be a person's undoing. The tissue was nearly mine. For all that I wanted the emptiness to go away, I didn't want him to be the one to hold me and feed me mindless platitudes.

He left when I told him to, and I laid there motionless looking up at the stars. The cold seeped into my bones reminding me of my continued mortality and I slipped one hand down into my knickers. Tears streamed down my face as I hit my release, my body shattering into a thousand slivers, each as bright as the stars above.

ZOOCHOROUS BY CHARLIE J FORREST

This is natural, I tell myself as the kettle begins to whistle.

It's called zoochorous in biology, I think. Either that or some other kind of zoo thing. Zoophilia? No, that's what those weirdos on TV who have sex with horses call themselves. No, zoochorous, definitely... maybe.

Plants really are amazing you see. They don't judge they don't spend their whole lives running ragged trying to find the one, the perfect mate to spread their genes with. No, they just chill out, lay back and let the universe take care of things.

I lift the kettle off the stove, pop open the spout and let it cool for a few minutes. Then, taking up my spoon, I start to pour it into the tube. I add a little at first, just enough to mix in with the powder into a clumpy paste. It's like making hot chocolate, I mean making real proper hot chocolate, trying to avoid those weird undissolved bergs of brown that stick to your lips.

It's ingenious really, the way plants do it. Just put everything they've got into their seeds and just let them go. They could all get vacuumed up and the tree wouldn't give a flying fuck it's still doing precisely what it thinks it should. But the other half, that's even more amazing. To just take genetic material from anywhere, just, fucking drifting out of the sky in some cases and go, "Hey, you know what, this'll probably do fine." I mean, people talk about nature versus nurture when it comes to sperm donations and single parents and stuff but, really, when you think about it. Reproducing without the slightest idea of who you're doing it with is actually pretty fucking natural.

I pour the last of the water in. The plaster mix reaches neatly up to the line but leaves a chunky gap before the end of the tube. My first is a blur stroking up and down my cock. I check that I've taped off the sharp edges, test the temperature with my free hand. All's good. Here we are old bean, time to put on a good show. I plunge myself into the tube of plaster trying to think of the sexiest thing I can… talk about performance anxiety!

Hell, even Jesus said "consider the lilies," dirty fucker that he was.

The next day I get to the park extra early. Hiding in the bushes is a bit of a cliché but I like to think I at least do a proper job of it. I wriggle over the railings before dawn, find the usual spot next to the brook. The entrenching tool makes easy work of the loose topsoil and the camo netting and army surplus combats make me hard to spot, even if I'm not exactly comfortable.

She arrives just before seven, bang on time. And as always her golden retriever makes his usual tour of the park, sniff this bin, that tree, come over to these bushes. I reach out, a scrap of bacon in my palm, He licks it up eagerly, just enough time for me to clip the little parcel to his collar. Then she calls him and he's gone, the brown paper lump swinging wildly with his bounds.

"Good boy!" I whisper.

I love getting back to nature.

ABOUT THE AUTHORS

THE KINKY BRITS

"Spankingly good erotica from a collective of kinky British writers."

Find out more at: http://thekinkybrits.com/
Follow them on Twitter: @TheKinkyBrits
Find them on Facebook: /thekinkybrits

ANNA SKY

Anna is a corset-loving, tea-drinking kinky British erotica writer who bends naughty words to her will!

Find out more at: http://www.iamannasky.com/
Follow her on Twitter: @iamannasky
Find her on Facebook: /AnnaSkyErotica
Amazon UK: amazon.co.uk/Anna-Sky/e/B00FBS5OU2/
Amazon US: amazon.com/Anna-Sky/e/B00FBS5OU2/

CHARLIE J FORREST

Writer, rigger, well-dressed pervert

Find out more at: http://cjforrest.com/
Follow him on Twitter: @CJForrestauthor
Find him on Facebook: /cjforrestauthor
Amazon UK: amazon.co.uk/Charlie-J-Forrest/e/B00I3BG7B4/
Amazon US: amazon.com/Charlie-J-Forrest/e/B00I3BG7B4/

LOLA SPARKLES

Lola is a voracious reader of smut who has a handy way with words.

Follow her on Twitter: @lolasparkles82

Printed in Poland
by Amazon Fulfillment
Poland Sp. z o.o., Wrocław